Hanna-Barbera
SCOOBY DOO...
WHERE ARE YOU!

Ottenheimer Publishers, Inc.

It's beginning to rain, Scooby.

We're in luck. There's a cave.

There's nothing worse than being caught in the rain.

Look! Up in the sky. It's a bird. It's a plane.

It's a witch.

And it's also time to get out of here!

VRROOOMM

I once ate dinner with the Queen of England.

If he ate dinner with the Queen, I'm the King.

Gulp!
He told the truth.

I'll catch that stupid Mystery Machine this time.

Hey, did any of you guys see somebody standing on the corner waving at us?

Nope.
He was more like *spinning*.

ZOOP

Good night, Scooby.
Have pleasant dreams.

In this place? She must be a real...

...optimist.

What's up?

A monster is coming?   Yeah.

Then we're leaving.

I'm going to take Scooby's picture for the "Cute Puppy News".

"Cute Puppy News?"

What happened, Daphne?

I'm not sure but I don't think Scooby identifies with cute puppies anymore.

You can say that again.

It moved? That's only your imagination, Scooby.

Yiii!

I've got terrific imagination.
I hope.

This is a nice quiet beach for a nap. Zzzz.

Ouch!

We're lucky we didn't pick a busy beach.

Too late.

The mummy's gone!

Where could it be?

When you find it, let me know.

Oh, oh!
We're in real trouble.

We've got to get across the river and there's no bridge. What can we do?

Where there's a will, there's a way. Sailing, sailing, over the bounding main.

Careful, Velma. Scooby's going to scare you.

BOOO!

Yikes!

Relax, Scooby. That was you.

Scooby, I'd like you to meet a real witch.

If she's a real witch, then...

...I'm a real chicken.

Let's get out of here! Yiiii!

Are you frightened, Scooby?

Me? Frightened? Not at all.

Neither am I.

I changed my mind.

Wait for me!

I need a volunteer to go into the haunted house.

Volunteer?

That's a long word that means *me!*

A mirage pirate ship!

And mirage pirates!

Now that's the kind
of mirage I like.

Why are you driving
so fast, Fred?

I forgot Scooby at the
drive-in restaurant.

Oh, poor Scooby.

Are you all right,
Scooby?

Are you kidding?

Help!
Get out of here!

The mighty Mad Monster
is coming to town in a rage.

And the mini Mystery
Machine is leaving in
a hurry.

It's time for Scooby to go to bed.

Who, me?

Where are you going?

To bed.

That's not what she meant.

Last one in the pool is a rotten egg.

Ouch!

Yeow!

Remind me to fill the pool next time.

What next time?

Sea air sure keeps those jaws busy.

What was that?

I shouldn't have mentioned *jaws*.

How did you dig
so deep, so fast.

It was very simple.

I didn't.

The mighty hunter runs
like a race horse...

...leaps like a lion...

...and is yellow
like a chicken.

I'll go first.

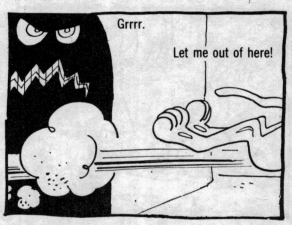

Grrrr.

Let me out of here!

I said I'd go first.

Scooby found a bone.

You're a good bone hunter, Scooby.

But this is ridiculous.

What is it, Scooby?

Hmm, a house for rent. Really cheap.

Now I know why it's cheap. It's haunted.

Scooby's feelings will
be hurt if he can't help.

Don't feel bad, Scooby.

To tell the truth,
I don't mind at all.

He won't catch me.

Ha ha ha!
You can't get out.

Ha ha ha!
You can too.

Good evening.

Gulp.

May I have one little bite?

Yeow!

You certainly may.

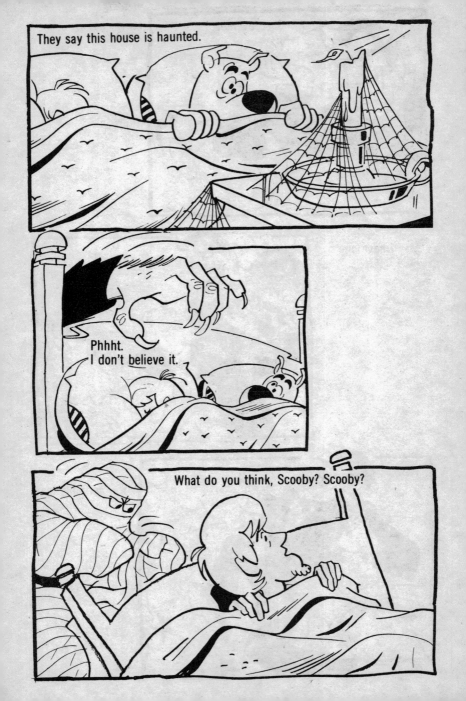

A haunted castle!

When should we investigate?

How about next year!

I want to
go faster!

O.k., Shaggy.

I wonder if that's
fast enough?

A little thunder
doesn't bother me.

But a lot of lightning
sure does.

I wonder if anyone's home in this haunted house?

There's nobody here but us monsters.

Yeooow!

EXIT

Hey, look!
Cotton candy!

I wonder if it works?

It works.

Fred has to see a doctor.

Come in, the doctor will be happy to see all of you.

You didn't say your doctor was Dr. Frankenstein, Fred.

A treasure chest!

How do I open it?

Yii!
How do you close it?

There's supposed to be a ghost Indian village around here.

I'll believe it when I see it.

Why are you turning around.

I see it! I see it!

vvVOOOMMM

I wonder if anyone's home?

Ullp!

This is where I came in, folks.